A Happy Day® Book Collection

My Special Easter Stories

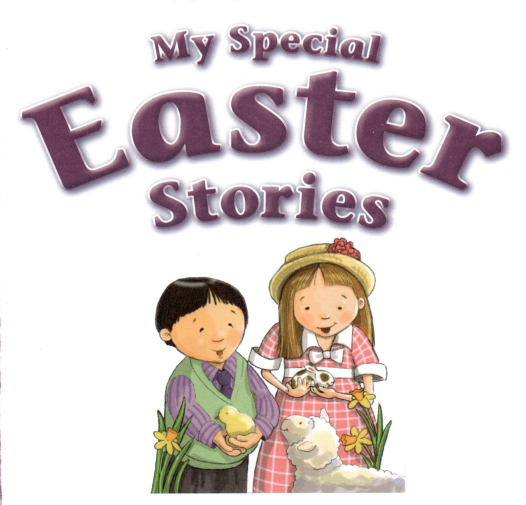

Cincinnati, Ohio

A Happy Day® Book Collection

Compilation copyright © 2013 by Standard Publishing.

Breakfast with Jesus copyright © 2012 by Standard Publishing
A Child's Story of Easter copyright © 2006 by Standard Publishing
Easter Surprises copyright © 2007 by Standard Publishing
Amazing Miracles of Jesus copyright © 2012 by Standard Publishing
My Story of Jesus copyright © 2001, 2005 by Standard Publishing
Let's Celebrate Jesus on Easter copyright © 2004 by Standard Publishing
Jesus Lives! The Easter Story copyright © 1999, 2005 by Standard Publishing

Published by Standard Publishing, Cincinnati, Ohio, www.standardpub.com. Compilation copyright © 2013 by Standard Publishing. All rights reserved. #35891. Manufactured in Thailand, January 2013. No part of this book may be reproduced in any form, except for brief quotations in reviews, without the written permission of the publisher. Happy Day® is a registered trademark of Standard Publishing. Printed in Thailand. Cover design: Dale Meyers

ISBN: 978-0-7847-3683-8

18 17 16 15 14 13   1 2 3 4 5 6 7 8 9

Contents

Breakfast with Jesus
By Mark A. Taylor; *Illustrated by* Scott Burroughs

A Child's Story of Easter
By Susan Hardesty; *Illustrated by* Christina Stephenson and Terry Julien

Easter Surprises
By Laura Derico; *Illustrated by* Phyllis Harris

Amazing Miracles of Jesus
By Charlotte Adelsperger; *Illustrated by* Nancy Munger

My Story of Jesus
By Jennifer Holder; *Illustrated by* Nancy Munger

Let's Celebrate Jesus on Easter
By Amy Beveridge; *Illustrated by* Rusty Fletcher

Jesus Lives! The Easter Story
By Laura Derico; *Illustrated by* Ronda Krum

Breakfast with Jesus

"I'm cold," said Thomas, as the night breeze blew across his wet arms.

"Me too," said Nathanael, and he shivered in the creaky boat.

"I'm hungry," said James, as he watched the water and their empty fishing net.

"Me too," said John, and his stomach growled and rumbled.

All the fishermen laughed—

—all except Peter.

"Keep fishing!" he commanded. "It's almost morning, and we haven't caught a thing." Peter sighed.

"I wish Jesus were here," he said to himself. "I hope we'll see him again soon."

Just then the fishermen heard a voice from far away.

The fishermen didn't know what to think. They didn't know what to say. They peered through the fog and saw a man on the land.

"Do you have any fish?" the man called again.

"No," said Thomas and Nathanael, James and John.

"No," said Peter.

"No!" said all the cold and hungry fishermen again from their creaky boat on the quiet lake.

And then the man said something quite surprising . . .

"Throw your net on the other side of the boat."

Thomas looked at Nathanael.
James looked at John.
They all looked at Peter.
And Peter said, "OK, let's try it."

The fishermen tugged the heavy net out of the water and into the boat. Not one fish. Then they heaved the net back into the water on the other side of the boat.

"There," said Thomas. "We did what he said. But what difference does it make? We'll never catch any fish tonight."

And then it happened!

FISH!
The net was full of fish!
Swimming, flipping, flopping fish!
The net bulged and almost broke. The men could not haul it back into the boat.

John stared across the water at the man still watching from the shore.

"It's Jesus," he said. ***"It's Jesus!*** Jesus is the one who told us where to fish!"

"I want to see him!" said Peter.
Peter dove into the lake.

Plop, ker-plop!

"Before Jesus died, he told us he would meet us!" he remembered as he swam. Left arm, right arm!

"Jesus told us he would live forever!" Kick hard! Hurry, hurry!

"Jesus died once, but never again!"

Peter smiled as he sloshed out of the water and onto the shore. There was Jesus, cooking fish over a small fire.

Soon the other fishermen brought the boat to land, dragging their net full of fish.

"Come and have breakfast with me," Jesus said.

Jesus gave them bread and fish to eat.
"Thank you, God, for our food," he said.
"Thank you for my fishermen friends.
Thank you for loving us."

Now Thomas and Nathanael were warm, sitting by the fire Jesus made.

And James and John were full, eating the tasty breakfast Jesus cooked.

And Peter—well, Peter sat on the seashore and munched his breakfast and talked with Jesus all morning long.

He couldn't have been happier!

The time had come to celebrate a great festival. A crowd of people started waving palm branches and laying them in the street. A very special guest was coming to the city to celebrate.

It was Jesus!

Where is Jesus?
What animal is Jesus riding into the city?
Do the people look happy or sad to see Jesus?
What color are the palm branches?

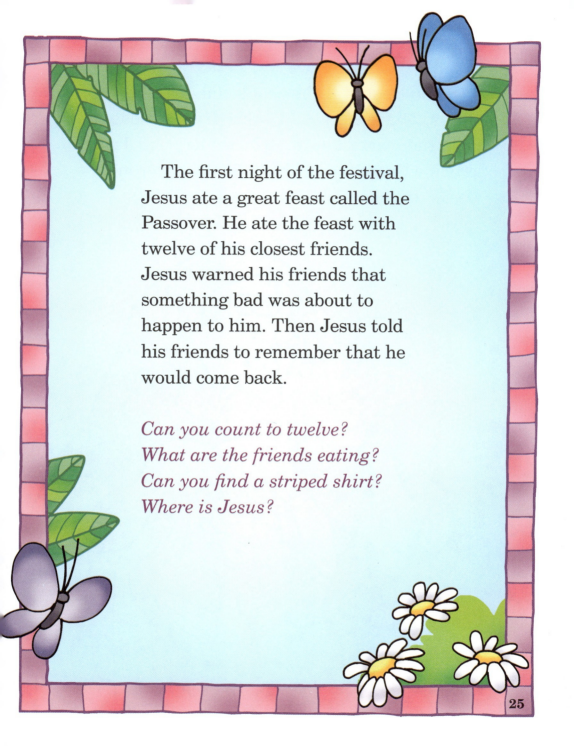

The first night of the festival, Jesus ate a great feast called the Passover. He ate the feast with twelve of his closest friends. Jesus warned his friends that something bad was about to happen to him. Then Jesus told his friends to remember that he would come back.

Can you count to twelve?
What are the friends eating?
Can you find a striped shirt?
Where is Jesus?

Some leaders of the people did not like Jesus. The leaders paid Jesus' friend Judas to help them arrest Jesus. The leaders had Jesus crucified even though he did nothing wrong. Jesus' friends were sad.

What are the leaders giving Judas?
How many crosses are on this page?

One man named Joseph was very sad because he loved Jesus. Joseph owned a cave called a tomb. Joseph and others who loved Jesus buried Jesus' body in the empty tomb. Then a big stone was rolled over to cover the doorway to the tomb.

Point to the big stone that covers the doorway.
What shape is the stone?
Where is Jesus?
What color is the jar that the woman is carrying?

The leaders who did not like Jesus were afraid because Jesus had said he would be back. The leaders ordered guards to stand watch at Jesus' tomb. The guards stood in front of the big stone that covered the tomb.

Where is the tomb?
How many soldiers are guarding the tomb?
What is covering the tomb?
Who is buried inside it?

Three days later some women went to visit Jesus' tomb early in the morning. A wonderful surprise was waiting for them there—the big stone was moved away from the entrance, and Jesus was not there!

He was alive!

What are the women holding?
Point to the tomb where Jesus had been buried.
Where is the stone now?
Where is Jesus?

Later Jesus came to his friends while they were fishing. Jesus appeared to his friends on the beach because he wanted to show them that he was alive—just like he said he would be!

Jesus told them to go tell everyone the good news!

What are Jesus' friends cooking?
Where is Jesus?
What color is Jesus' robe?
How many friends are with Jesus?

Our friend Jesus is alive today! Jesus loves it when you talk to him. Jesus loves for you to tell others about him.

Go into all the world and preach the Good News to everyone. —Mark 16:15

Easter Surprises

Mrs. Hen sits on her nest,
cozy and warm,
on a quiet Easter morning.
She cocks her head . . . what does she hear?

Crack, crackle, creak . . . peek!
A surprise has come for Mrs. Hen
on a happy Easter morning.

How many chicks do you see?

Mr. Bunny stretches and yawns.
He sniffs and listens
in the sweet Easter morning.
He lifts his ears . . . what does he hear?

Hop, hop, hop . . . flop!
It's a surprise for Mr. Bunny
on a busy Easter morning.

How many bunnies do you see?

Mrs. Sheep walks along,
warming her wool
in the sunny Easter morning.
She shakes her head . . . what does she hear?

Bounce, leap, bobble . . . bleat!
A surprise has come for Mrs. Sheep
on this lively Easter morning.

How many lambs do you see?

Mr. Goose waddles to the pond,
flapping his wings
in the misty Easter morning.
And under his wings . . . what does he see?

Wiggle, splish, wobble . . . splash!
Surprises swim around Mr. Goose
on this bright Easter morning.

How many goslings do you see?

Flowers open to the sun
on a shiny Easter morning.
And there on a stem . . . what do you see?

Mary slips silently down the path
in the early morning.
She goes to the tomb . . . what does she see?

Who is in the tomb?

She looks, she listens, she turns—she sees!
Jesus is not dead. He is alive!
On this first Easter morning.

Little children,
in a colorful row,
in church this Easter morning.
They're so happy . . . what do they do?

Smile, stand, shout . . . sing!
They know it's no surprise—

How many children do you see?

Jesus who died is now alive,
on this and every morning!

The angel said, "Do not be so surprised.
You are looking for Jesus, the Nazarene,
*   who was crucified.*
He isn't here! He has been raised
*   from the dead!"*
*   —Mark 16:6*

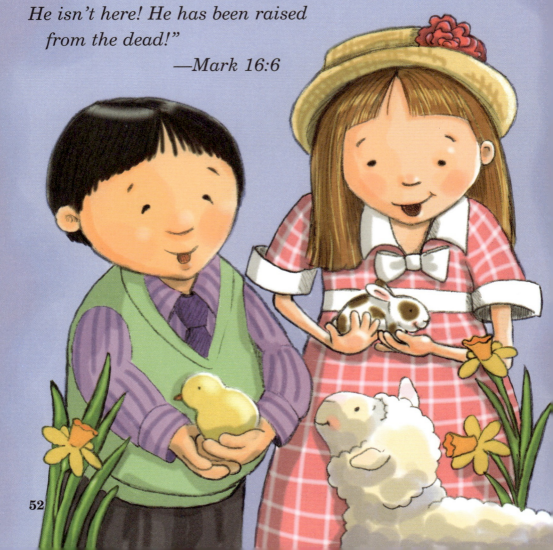

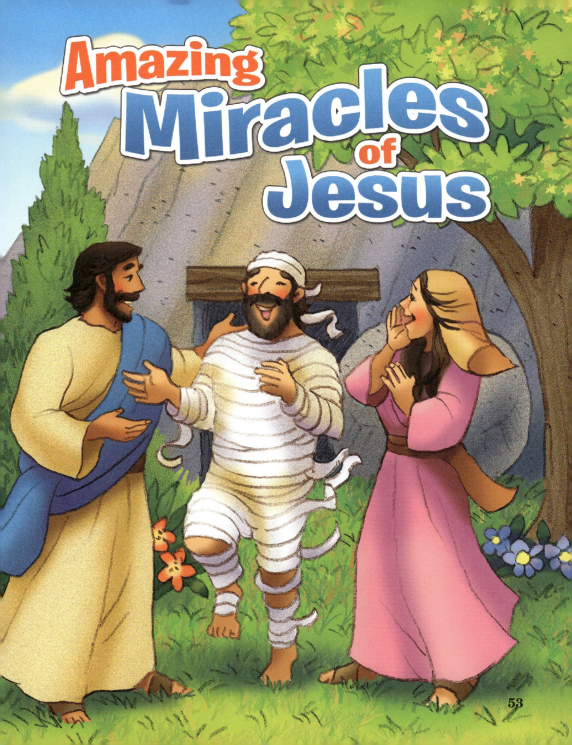

Jesus, God's only Son, was full of wonderful love and great power. To show us he was God's Son, Jesus did many amazing miracles while he was on earth.

A man with a bad skin disease knelt before Jesus. "If you want to, you can make me well," he said. Jesus' eyes shone with love. He put his hand on the man. "Be healed!" Jesus said.

The man's skin looked like new!

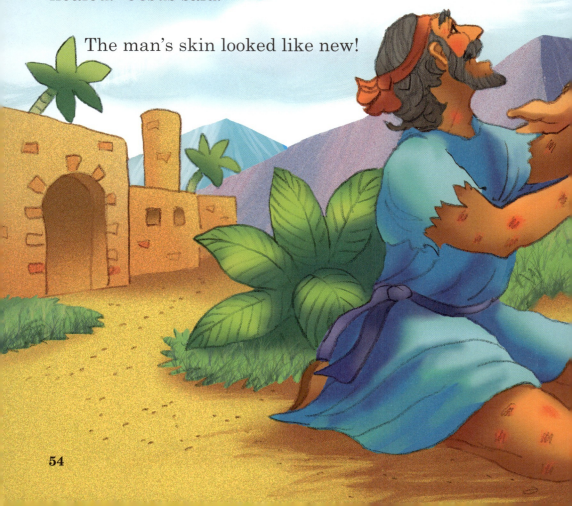

A woman had been bleeding for twelve years. No doctors could help her. *If I can just touch Jesus' clothes, I will be healed,* she thought. She followed Jesus in the crowd and touched a fringe of his robe. Her bleeding stopped!

Jesus could tell that someone had been healed. "Who touched my clothes?" he asked. The woman told him what she had done, and Jesus smiled. "Your faith has made you well. Go in peace," he said.

A government official found Jesus in the town of Cana. "My son is very sick! He may die!" he cried. "Please come heal him!"

Jesus said, "Go back home. Your son will live."

When the father got home, he learned that his son was alive and well! The fever had disappeared the very hour Jesus said the boy would live. Jesus showed God's power over sickness.

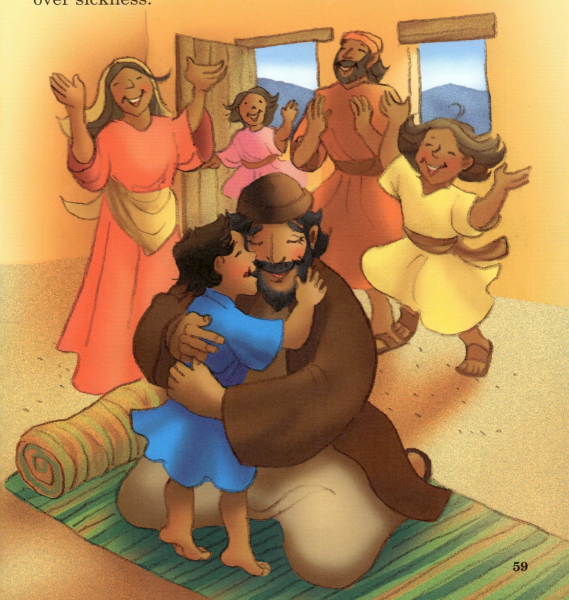

Huge crowds followed Jesus. They listened to his teaching and felt his love. Many believed he was the Son of God.

Friends brought a man with an evil spirit to Jesus. The man was blind and couldn't speak. Jesus showed God's power over evil. The man became calm and could see and speak!

Simon and his friends fished all night in the Sea of Galilee, but they didn't catch anything. The next day Jesus told them, "Take your boat where it is deeper." They doubted they would catch any fish, but they did what Jesus said.

Jesus showed God's power over nature. The men's nets became so full of fish that they began to tear! Then Simon knew Jesus was from God, so he and two other fishermen became disciples, or special followers, of Jesus.

Jesus' disciples were in a boat far out on a lake. Strong winds blew, and big waves splashed over the boat. Then the disciples saw Jesus walking on the water toward them! "I am here! Don't be afraid!" he called out.

Peter shouted to Jesus, "If it is really you, I want to come to you!" Peter started to walk on the waves, but he began to sink. "Save me!" he yelled. Jesus grabbed him. "Why did you not believe?" Jesus asked when they got into the boat.

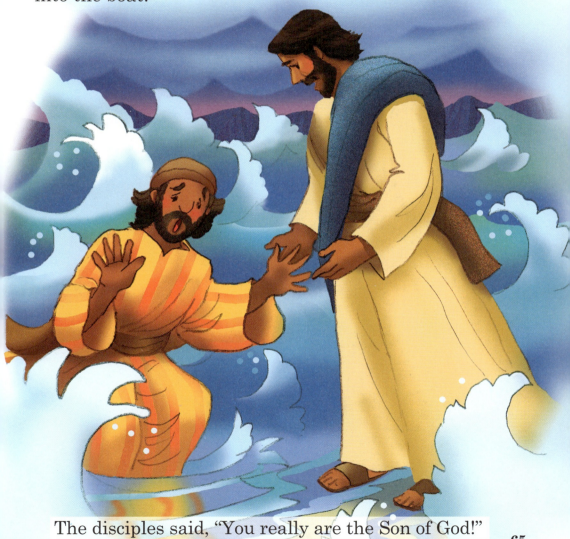

The disciples said, "You really are the Son of God!"

Jesus' friend Lazarus lived in Bethany with his sisters, Mary and Martha. One day Lazarus became very sick and died. Mary and Martha wished Jesus had been there to heal their brother. They cried when Lazarus was put in a grave.

Four days later Jesus came to Bethany. "Your brother will rise again," he said to Martha with a kind voice.

While he was near the tomb, Jesus' eyes filled with tears. He prayed to his heavenly Father and shouted, "Lazarus, come out!" Lazarus walked out alive! Jesus showed God's power over death!

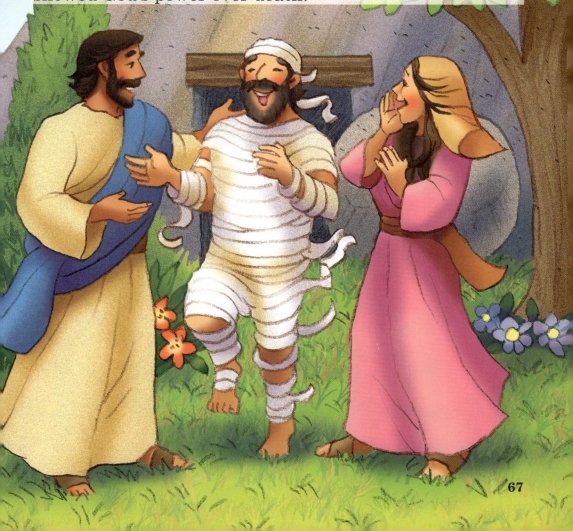

Enemies put Jesus to death on a cross. Three days later some women came to his tomb, but Jesus was not there. An angel told them, "Jesus has risen, just as he said he would!"

It was the most amazing miracle!

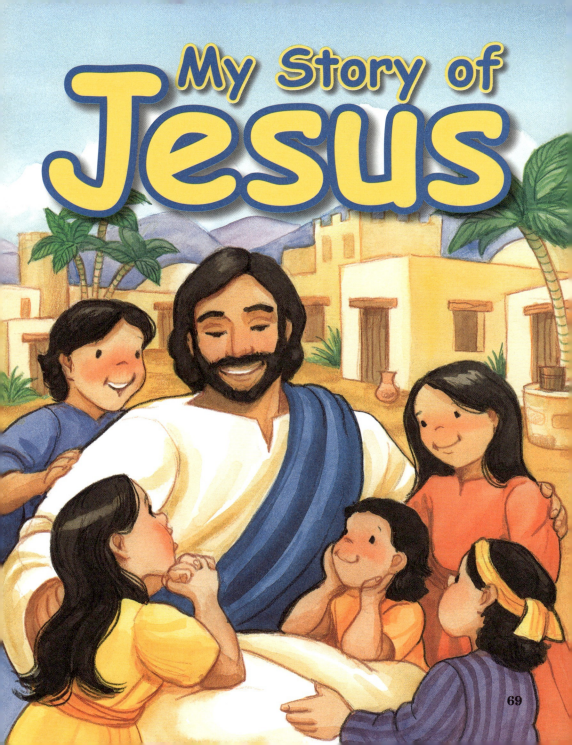

Long ago God said that he would send his Son to be the Savior and King of his people.

God's Son, Jesus, was born in Bethlehem. His mother, Mary, wrapped him in cloths and laid him in a manger.

As Jesus grew up, he obeyed his parents and pleased God. When he was 12, Jesus talked with the priests and teachers about God's teachings and God's love. They were amazed at how much Jesus understood.

A man named John was telling people about Jesus. "Good news!" he said. "God has sent Jesus to save us. We need to get ready for him!" People came to John to be baptized.

Jesus came to be baptized too. When Jesus came up from the water, God's Spirit came from Heaven like a dove. Then a voice from Heaven said, "You are my Son. I love you. I am pleased with you."

Then Jesus began to do the work God had planned for him.

Jesus showed God's care and concern for people. He made sick people well and made blind people see again. He even made lame people able to walk!

Jesus showed God's power. One day when Jesus and some of his followers were in a boat, a terrible storm came up.

The followers were afraid, but Jesus told the wind and waves, "Quiet! Be still!" And the storm stopped.

Jesus became known as a wonderful teacher. Mothers and fathers brought their children to Jesus so he could bless them and pray for them. Jesus told stories to help people understand his teaching.

Jesus went to Jerusalem and ate the Passover meal with his followers. He told them he would leave them soon.

Then Jesus showed his followers a special way to always remember him. He gave thanks to God, broke bread, and passed it to his followers. He passed his cup to them too. "Remember me when you eat this bread and drink from this cup," said Jesus.

Jesus was ready to finish the work that God had planned for him. That meant he must die. This was part of God's plan for saving people from sin.

Jesus died on a cross. His followers were very sad. They buried Jesus' body in a tomb and closed it with a heavy stone.

But when some women went back to Jesus' tomb, they were surprised to find the stone was rolled away and the tomb was empty!

Suddenly, an angel appeared. "Jesus is not here," the angel told the women. "He is alive again!"

Many people saw Jesus after he had risen. Jesus told his followers, "Go everywhere and tell everyone the good news about me!"

Jesus returned to Heaven to make a new home for his followers. But he promised to come back again one day. What a happy day that will be!

At Easter
I will decorate eggs
with lots of bright colors . . .

But Jesus is the one who colors my world every day.

The heavens tell of the glory of God! —Psalm 19:1

At Easter
I will buy sweet treats
to share with my friends . . .

But Jesus is the one who shares all my thoughts and feelings.

You know my every thought. —Psalm 139:2

At Easter
I will hunt for eggs . . .

Every moment you know where I am. —Psalm 139:3

At Easter
I see new life all around me . . .

But Jesus' new life on that first Easter morning is what I celebrate.

He isn't here! He has risen from the dead! —Luke 24:6

On Easter
I will dress in new clothes
and get a basket full of surprises...

But knowing Jesus loves me is the best gift I will ever receive.

The free gift of God is eternal life through Christ Jesus our Lord. —Romans 6:23

Yes, Easter is filled with good things bright and new . . .

But I can praise Jesus for giving me new life every day of the year!

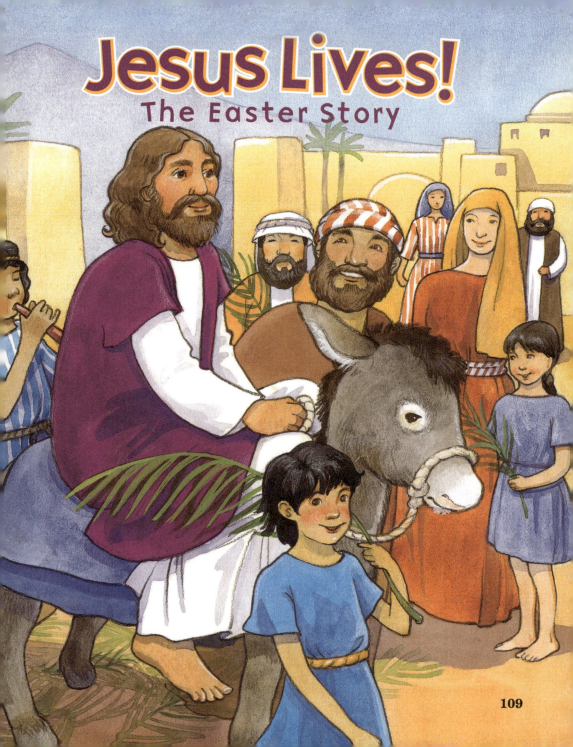

The King is coming!" the people shouted. A large crowd gathered to see Jesus.

Soon Jesus came into the city of Jerusalem, riding on a young donkey.

"Hosanna in the highest!" the people shouted to Jesus. "Blessed is he who comes in the name of the Lord!"

Jesus and his disciples went to the upper room of a house in the city to celebrate Passover together. As the meal was being served, Jesus wrapped a towel around his waist.

He took a bowl of water and began washing the feet of all of his disciples. When he was finished, Jesus said, "Follow my example. You should serve others just as I serve you."

During the meal, Jesus reminded the disciples that he would soon leave them. He took bread, gave thanks to God, broke it, and gave it to his disciples. He also took the cup, gave thanks, and gave it to his disciples.

Jesus said, "I'm giving this bread and cup to you. Remember me whenever you eat bread and drink from the cup together."

When they had finished the meal, they sang a song of worship to God and went to the Mount of Olives.

Jesus and his disciples went to a garden to pray. Jesus took Peter, James, and John with him and said, "My heart is heavy because I am so sad. Stay here with me."

Then Jesus went a little farther by himself and prayed to God, "Father, I will do whatever you want me to do."

Jesus prayed this prayer three times. Each time, he went back and found his disciples sleeping, because they were very tired. The third time, Jesus woke them, saying, "Let's go! The one who will betray me is here!"

Judas Iscariot had been one of Jesus' friends. But now he came with men to arrest Jesus.

They took Jesus to the high priest to be judged. Some people were angry that Jesus said he was the Son of God. They didn't believe Jesus, even though he only spoke the truth.

No one could find anything bad that Jesus had done. Even the governor, Pilate, wanted to set him free. But the crowds shouted, "Crucify him!" So Pilate turned Jesus over to the soldiers to be crucified.

Jesus was quiet. He knew this was part of his Father's plan.

The soldiers took Jesus away. They dressed him like a king, with a purple robe and a crown of thorns. They made fun of Jesus. They did not understand that the kingdom Jesus talked about was not like earthly kingdoms. It was the kingdom of God!

They led Jesus to a place called Calvary. There they crucified him with two criminals, one on his right and one on his left.

But Jesus still loved the people. From the cross, he said, "Father, forgive them. They do not know what they are doing."

Darkness came over the whole land. With his last breath, Jesus cried out, "Father, I put myself in your hands!" Then he died.

The earth shook and rocks split. The men who were guarding Jesus said, "He really was the Son of God!"

A rich man named Joseph was a follower of Jesus. He asked Pilate for Jesus' body so he could bury him. He placed Jesus' body in a new tomb and rolled a big stone in front of the entrance.

Some of the leaders of the people were afraid that Jesus' friends would come to take his body out of the tomb. So Pilate sent guards to the tomb to seal it and watch it.

At dawn on the first day of the week, Mary Magdalene and some women went to the tomb. They wanted to put spices on Jesus' body, as was the custom of their people.

But when the women arrived at the tomb, they were amazed! An angel of God had rolled the stone away and was sitting there. He was bright like a lightning flash and his clothes were as white as snow.

The angel said to the women, "Do not be afraid. Jesus is not here. He has risen, just as he said. Jesus lives!"

The women were so happy that they ran to tell all Jesus' disciples. The disciples were amazed. Could Jesus really be alive?

YES! JESUS LIVES!
Jesus appeared to the women and to his other disciples many times. He wanted to show them that he was alive so they could tell others.

He told them, "Go and tell all nations about me. Baptize them in the name of the Father, Son, and Holy Spirit. Teach them to obey everything I have told you. I promise that I will always be with you."

The disciples believed Jesus and did what he said. They were filled with joy, knowing that . . .

JESUS LIVES!